For Marrae Delilah Aiquier —J.M.

Thank you, God.
Dedicated to Yurie —S.E.

Text copyright © 2002 by Jean Marzollo
Illustrations copyright © 2002 by Shane W. Evans
All rights reserved. For information address
Jump at the Sun, 114 Fifth Avenue,
New York, New York 10011-5690.
Printed in Hong Kong
First Jump at the Sun paperback edition, 2003
   3 5 7 9 10 8 6 4
This book is set in 26-point BBGothic.
ISBN 0-7868-1758-5 (paperback)
A hardcover edition of *Shanna's Ballerina Show* is available from
Jump at the Sun/Hyperion Books for Children.
Library of Congress Cataloging-in-Publication Data on file.

Welcome to the SHANNA SHOW!
Take your seats, here we go!

SHANNA'S
Ballerina
SHOW

by **Jean Marzollo**
Illustrated by **Shane W. Evans**

JUMP AT THE SUN
HYPERION PAPERBACKS FOR CHILDREN
New York

I'm a ballerina.

**Wonder how
I know?**

I'll give you **5** clues on today's Shanna Show.

Clue 1: costume.
Leotard, tights.

And a fancy, dancy tutu
for performing under lights.

Clue 2: ballet shoes.
Soft, blue, and sweet.

They make me feel so la-di-da
and look so pretty on my feet.

And now we find we have arrived at Clue Number 3.
You'll need to get a ticket if you want a seat to see.

You say you want to see a show?
You say you want a treat?
Admission is a penny.
Here's your ticket. Take a seat.

Clue 4: music.
Hear it sing! Hear it soar!

**Watch the movement of my arms
as I leap across the floor!**

If you want a seat to see,
get a ticket: that's **3**.

Fare thee well,
it's time to go.